To Scout
With love, CK

For Paul, Howie and Kitty
With love, SH

The Problem with Pierre

Text © C K Smouha
Illustrations © Suzanna Hubbard

British Library Cataloguing-in-Publication Data.

A CIP record for this book is available from the British Library.
ISBN: 978-1-908714-85-5
First published in the UK, 2020 and USA, 2021

Cicada Books Ltd
48 Burghley Road
London, NW5 1UE
www.cicadabooks.co.uk

Printed in China

THE PROBLEM WITH PIERRE

G.K.Smouha

illustrated by

Suzanna Hubbard

cicada

Bertram and Alan were next-door neighbours.
They were also great friends.

They were also very, very different to one another.

Bertram was neat as a pin. 'A place for everything and everything in its place,' said Bertram.

Alan was not very neat. In fact, he was extremely messy. 'Everything shines when things aren't perfect,' said Alan.

Bertram loved his house, but he couldn't shake the feeling that something was missing.

'Maybe you should change your sofa,' said Alan,
'that one looks very uncomfortable.'
'No it's not that,' said Bertram. 'I need some company.'

So Bertram got a cat called Pierre.

Pierre was a fine cat, with marble-blue eyes
and a haughty air. 'He's perfect for me,'
thought Bertram.

But Pierre was not so sure.

He did not want to eat out of Bertram's finest china bowl.

He did not want to sleep in the fancy cat bed that Bertram had bought.

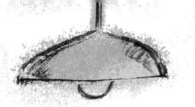

And he *definitely* did not want to sit on Bertram's sofa.

What could be the problem with Pierre?

Pierre preferred Alan's house.
He would climb through the
window that never
quite closed...

Snack on Alan's leftover scraps of dinner...

Curl up for a nap on Alan's old sheepskin coat...

...and when he had rested, he would stretch his legs, saunter over, tuck himself next to Alan on the beat-up old sofa, and the two of them would watch telly together.

Bertram was not happy.

Alan did not like to see his friend upset.
'Why don't you borrow my sheepskin coat?'
he said.

So Bertram put the sheepskin coat on the floor and
Pierre curled up and promptly fell asleep.

But Pierre still wouldn't touch a morsel of food.
'He likes finding his own food to eat,' said Alan.
'You can borrow my bowl.'

So Bertram put some leftovers in the bowl, and when his back was turned,
Pierre leapt up onto the table and devoured the lot.

And so, Pierre ate and slept at Bertram's house, and in the evenings, he would trot over to Alan's house, curl up on the sofa and watch the telly.

At first, Bertram didn't mind. But the more he thought about it, the more it bothered him.

After all, the best thing about having a cat is
snuggling up togther and watching telly.

'Why don't you borrow my sofa?' said Alan.
'Are you sure?' asked Bertram.
'Absolutely,' said Alan.

So Bertram got rid of his uncomfortable sofa, and put Alan's beat-up old sofa in its place.

He took a seat. 'Oh this really is quite comfortable,' he thought. Pierre hopped straight into his lap and purred. At last Pierre was happy, and so was Bertram.

Almost. Something was niggling him.

Alan's living room just didn't feel right without the sofa.

He washed the dishes.

And tidied away the books.

He folded his clothes and put them neatly in the cupboard.

But the room still felt wrong.
It felt empty and sad.
Alan felt a little sad, too.

'That was a really good idea, Bertram,' said Alan.

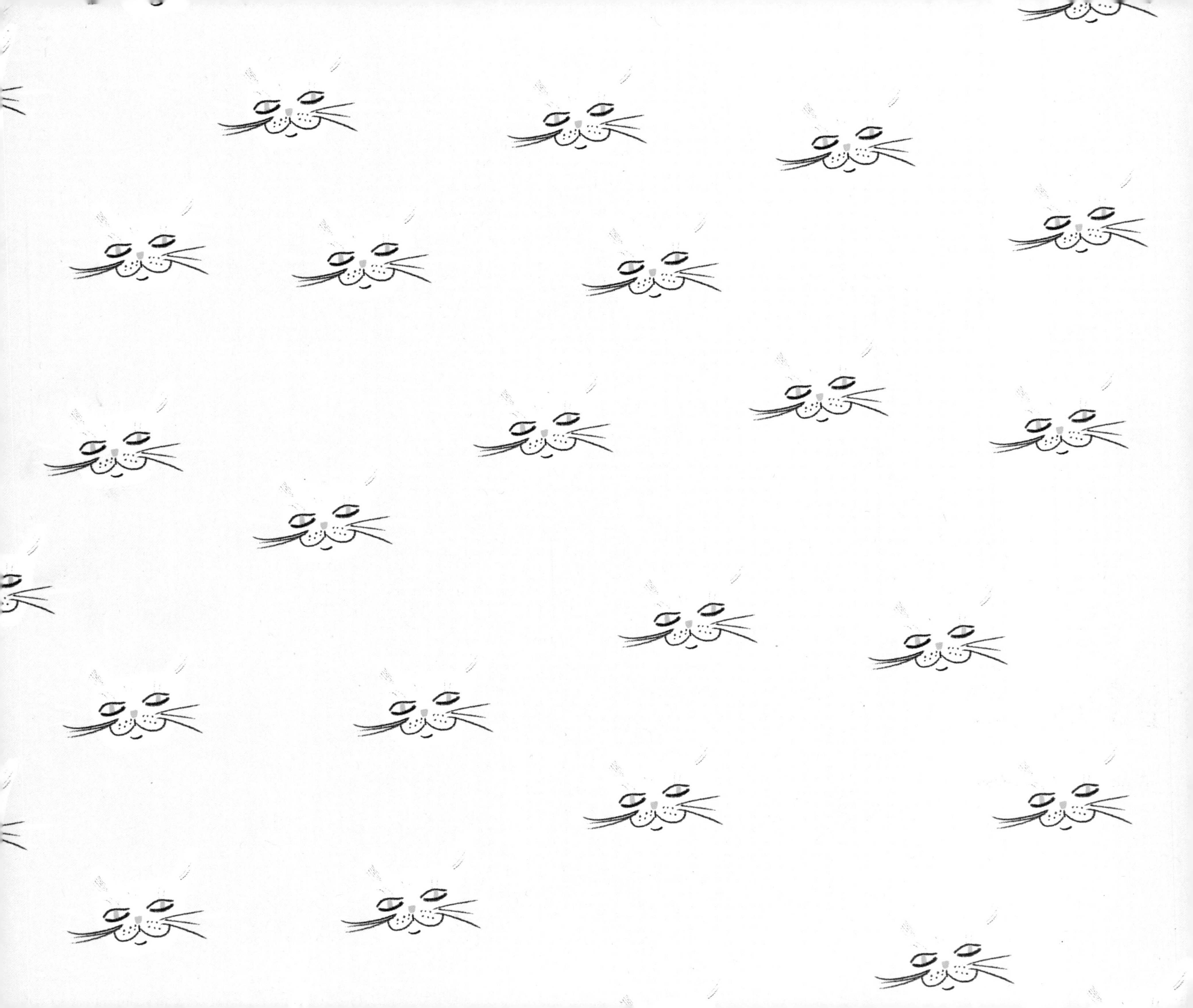